The

Ugliest Man

The Killing of
Janis Joplin

By

Martin Hancock

Background

On 4th October, 1970, Janis Joplin, probably the greatest female blues singer ever, died in a seedy motel room from a heroin over-dose. At just 27 years old, she had been famous for just 8 years; yet, in that short time, she challenged not only the music industry but also western society itself, and in particular, an almost global perception of what it meant to be a woman at that time. She remains an iconic figure in both her uncompromising stance on female sexuality and her refusal to be shackled by meaningless and outmoded convention.

But, she made mistakes. Drugs and booze were her coping mechanisms in a music business where achievement was, and still is, measured in the number of days since your last chart success.

And yet, there was something else that festered in Janis' heart and, ultimately, would be the emotional cancer that would bring her to that motel room where she died. One single event in her life would plant a seed of self-doubt that would grow into a towering presence in her mind. This play puts that event in its rightful place as a cruel and corrosive act and one that has been overlooked in terms of its significance for nearly forty years. Even an award-winning biography about Janis gives this singularly destructive experience little more than a paragraph. However, today, with the recognized power and influence of social media, we can re-evaluate this event in Janis' short life and see it for what it is worth.

Ultimately, Janis' story is a moral tale of how one of the most uncompromising, individual and creative people can be scythed down by something as apparently superficial as her own appearance. Janis' story exposes a fundamental truth that is even more important today than it was forty years ago. Respecting our differences is probably the most loving thing humans can do for each other.

The Ugliest Man

Characters

JANIS   Iconic Joplin clothes, including Ostrich Feathers. Aged about 25.

DOROTHY   Janis' 50+ year-old mother. Typical 1960s housewife apparel.

BRANDON,
LOUIS,   19 year-old frat boys. All from
FRANKLIN,   very wealthy backgrounds.
BEN

JON   An important boyfriend of Janis' now aged around 50.

BACKSTAGE ROADIE   Youngish, long-haired roadie . Aged Around 25-35ish.

JOHN COOKE   Janis' Driver/road manager. Aged 29.

ALBERT GROSSMAN   Janis' manager. Aged around 45.

ROBERT GORDON   Suited, short-haired, glasses. Janis' lawyer. Aged late 40s.

RUTH-ANN   A student from Janis' High School. Now in her late 40s.

PEARL   Close friend of Janis' during her recording years. A heroin addict at the time. Now in her mid-40s

HOTEL CLERK   Male or female role. Any age.

SCENE 1

BACK PROJECTION

<u>Text</u>: 'October 6, 1967- The Matrix, San Francisco.'
<u>Image</u>: Picture of Janis on stage.

Scene is a rather scruffy motel room after the gig.
The scene opens with lights off. Janis is standing stage rear
holding a flickering Zippo lighter. She's on the phone.

JANIS

(Shouting.)

Lights...lights!

(A pause, then mutters...)

Jesus H Christ!

(...then loudly into the phone...)

It's the lights, Mother. Ain't no power. The pigs. They pulled
the fuses...shut us down. It's...what? I can't hear you. Can you
hear me?

(Lights come on. She extinguishes the lighter.)

1

Thank the fuck.

(*Shouting into the phone.*)

Gotta go now, Mother. I'll...I'll write you, OK?

(*Pause.*)

What?

I said, I'll write you.

(*Pause.*)

Momma?

(*She stares at the phone and then slams it back in the cradle.*)

Fuck, fuck, fuck!

Janis grabs a bottle of Southern Comfort off her dressing table and takes a long swig. Replacing it, she runs her hand through her hair and approaches centre stage front. There is an invisible mirror hanging there. She fiddles with her hair and then proceeds to pull various contortions with her face. Then she turns sideways and looks herself over. She grabs her breasts and hoists them up before giving up and slouching.

Jesus Christ! Who gives a shit?

She takes a cigarette from her dressing table and lights it with the Zippo. Then, seeing the mirror again, she approaches it. She adopts a coy facial expression and, speaking in a 'little girl' voice, holds a make-believe phone to her ear.

Hi, Mother. Yeah, it's me, Janis. How'ya doin'?
Oh, I'm OK. You know...doin'...fine. My hair? Yeah, I'm just off to the hair salon. Gonna get me one of those...what they call 'em? Beehives? You know, all back-combed and lacquered an' all. What's that? Clothes? Well, you know what? Yesterday, I bought this cute little number. Tight bodice, flared skirt, and you should see the print. Big flowers all over it. Made me look like...I dunno...like a bridesmaid or somethin'.
What? Boyfriend? No, no boyfriend, Mother.

(Shouting aggressively into the make-believe phone...)

I'm just too busy drinkin' and fuckin' anyone who's got space for a dick in their pants.

(Pause. Back with the sweet voice.)

You too, Mother.

(Covers her face with her hands.)

Shit! Shit! Shit!

(She aggressively addresses the mirror again, or perhaps it's the audience.)

You know your problem, girl? You let them fuck with your head, man. You open the door to your mind an' they all jus' trample in and stomp all over...over...who you are. You know what? I...I...don't even know who I am. Janis Joplin. Who the fuck is that? Jus' some weird-looking Texas bitch who sings. You know what? Ya have to fit in to know who you are. Otherwise...if you don't fit...you're in a world of one. Just you...I mean me.

(A swig from the bottle.)

Ya know what? People, they ask me, what am I thinkin', when I'm up there singin'. I'll tell you, man. I ain't thinkin' nothin'. My head? It's one big empty place. All I've got goin' on is the band and my voice. All the crap? It gets re-packaged into the song. Like I've been cleansed. Yeah. Cleaned out like some old trash can. But you know what? Trash cans always get re-filled.

She takes another swig and a drag from the cigarette, then paces the room. She is emotional. Tears begin to fall.

4

Jesus! You know what? The fuckin' pigs shut us down. Pulled the fuses! People...they were havin' a good time. They were in it. Know what I mean? They were just lettin' it go, man. What's the problem? Some sweet people dancin'. What the fuck! Dancin' 'cos they love me. Cos I am loved.

(Janis starts quietly singing the opening words to 'Stay With Me'.)

Where did you go // when things went wrong baby?
Who did you run to // And find a shoulder to lay your head upon?

(She stops and sinks to the floor crying. Suddenly, she points, but it's not clear whether she's pointing at the mirror or the audience.)

What the hell are you lookin' at?

FADE OUT

SCENE CHANGE TRACK: **The Zombies: 'Time of the Season'**

SCENE 2

FADE UP – LIGHTS STAGE FRONT LEFT

BACK PROJECTION

<u>Text:</u> 'Recording for a radio station KOLE documentary on Port Arthur's belated honouring of Janis Joplin in 1988.' <u>Image:</u> Image of Janis during her High School years.

A 46 year-old woman from Janis' high-school is being interviewed by a KOLE journalist as part of Port Arthur's belated honouring of Janis in 1988. We do not hear the questions being asked – just her responses. Sitting in a chair, she attaches a lapel-microphone.

RUTH-ANN

Is that OK?

(She pats the microphone on her lapel, which causes the unseen sound-engineer to wince.)

Sorry.

Er...my name's Ruth-Ann and, sure, I knew Janis Joplin. Well, as much as anyone can claim back then. Most avoided her. She was real weird. One day she'd turn up wearin' a polyester twinset an' her hair in a bun, next she'd be wearin' cut-off jeans an' a tee-shirt. I mean, Port Arthur didn't react well to anyone you couldn't rely on to look the same one day to the next.

Can I ask a question? Is that alright?

OK, I was just thinkin', why are you diggin' up all this old stuff? Nineteen-sixty, that's a mighty long time to look back.

Right, OK. Well, I read that she never forgave us. Our High-School crowd. She came back, you know. The reunion. Nineteen-seventy. She died a few weeks later. Tragic. Anyone dies that young, it's a loss. Even someone like her.

What's that?

You know she weren't no looker and that's a fact. Can't be denied. But, you know what? There were plenty of us girls who'd never have made it onto a magazine cover. This was Texas, remember. Some of us come from heavy stock. We all tried to make the best of it. Those of us who didn't have those natural good looks. Make-up, a hair-do. A nice dress, that sort of thing. But not her! No Siree. I never seen her wear make-up once. And that hair! So wild you'd need a lasso to tame it.

Me? I don't recall bein' especially mean to her. Any more than the others. You know, girls can be mean-minded at that age. Spiteful like. When she came back, the reunion I mean, it was to, you know, flip us the bird. She'd made good. Said to a reporter somethin' about makin' fifty thousand a week while we were all scratching for a few dollars working in dry cleaners. But, you know what? Makin' fifty thousand a week don't make up for bein' dead at twenty-seven. Not in my book anyways.

Fifty thousand a day was it? Oh, well, I stand corrected. But the sentiment stays the same, just more so I reckon.

Yes Sir, I heard about that. Some dumb contest at university. What can I say? She attracted that sort of thing. She had a mouth on her. Make a Texas cowboy blush, that's for sure. A woman has to act pretty as well as appear pretty. I don't see much has changed since then. Seems to me we've come out the other side of those feminism years an' women are still paradin' round with everythin' they've got in ya face with a label sayin' check this out boys.

Eh?

Feminism? I read about that in the news. Let me tell you, Mister. Women today could learn a lot from us Texas females. Even in those days, you try anythin' on with a Texas girl, you gonna find yourself standin' with ya balls stuffed in your shirt pocket.

Beggin' ya pardon?

Right, well, thing is, you were either in or out. Trouble was, she wanted to be in, but on her terms. She wanted the best of both worlds. She wanted to be part of the crowd, the in crowd. But I'm guessin' we were too...ordinary. So, she decided to be out, on the outside, but that meant she was...I dunno...out on her own.

Sex? Well, I don't know if I want to be talking about that. But, I heard tell she was pretty free an' easy. Maybe if she attended church more, she'd have had more respect for herself. Never saw anythin' like that myself, mind you. Some girls thought sleepin' around made them popular...you know...with the guys. All I know is she played in some folk band.

(She leans closer and speaks in a stage whisper.)

I think those guys were strummin' more than just their instruments, if you get my meanin'.

You gettin' all this?

Married? I guess you're talkin' 'bout that guy...what was his name...?

Eh?

9

Yeah, Peter. I never met him, though he was supposed to have come to their house, the parents, I mean. Never saw him. I never understood that, you know, the getting hitched thing. Certainly not to him. I read later he was a two-timin' bastard, so good riddance to bad rubbish is what I say. She dodged a bullet if you ask me.

Jon?

Yeah, when she came back for the reunion. I heard about this Jon. Some friend who came with her was spillin' the beans on that. You know what? For my money, he was the one. Jon, I mean. Read stuff since, an' I was right... back then. She should have roped and hog-tied that boy an' maybe she's still be alive today. Incredible, but it seems like he really did love her.

What?

Let me tell you somethin'. That whole hippy thing? How'd it go? Tune in and drop out? I'm tellin' ya, it were nothin' but an excuse to avoid responsibilities in life. Take the beads and tie-dye off any of those long-haired layabouts an' you'd have found well-off, middle-class kids. Spoilt brats. Never saw any kids from poor backgrounds prancin' around in that film. They were all city kids from wealthy Christian homes.

What?

The film? The film of Woodstock. You must have seen it.

Eh?

Me? A hippy? Look, growin' up snipping the balls off pigs gives ya an outlook on life that can't be covered by patchouli oil an' a headband an' that's a fact.

Look, what I'm sayin' is...she was a rebel. Far as I know they were a good family. Her parents an' all. She never appreciated that. Like those middle-class kids at Woodstock. It was all livin' for the moment. My opinion is that she was...what's the word...//

//...yeah, self-obsessed. She just wanted everyone to like her, but she just wasn't likable. Know what I mean? Not at that time. Not with us. Not Port Arthur.

You're welcome. Am I gettin' paid for this?

FADE OUT

SCENE CHANGE TRACK: Janis Joplin: 'Cry Baby'

FADE UP

BACK PROJECTION

<u>Text</u>: '1962- An Alpha Phi Omega Fraternity House,
University of Texas during Janis' short attendance.'
<u>Image</u>: Picture of Janis in High School gown and mortar.

*The scene is a frat house at the University of Texas. Four Alpha
Phi Omega frat boys are discussing a plan to raise money for
charity. Brandon, Louis and Franklin are lounging around on a
sofa and an easy chair. Ben is standing stage front, his back to
the other three.*

BRANDON

Come on, guys! It's traditional. Everyone will love it.

LOUIS

Yeah. Teach those commies a lesson. I mean, why are
communists so ugly?

FRANKLIN

It's Stalin. Have you seen that dude?

LOUIS

He's dead, you numbskull! Hey, Jew-boy, you're reading twentieth century. When did Uncle Joe die?

(Ben is standing with his hands thrust into his pockets and staring at his feet.)

BEN

March, 1953.

LOUIS

Shit, really?

(Reflective pause.)

Anyway, he was one ugly mother. So was...what's his name...er...that Marxist dude.

BEN

Karl Marx?

LOUIS

No, you idiot. Christ! Don't you know anything? I mean the guy who started communism...Russian guy.

FRANKLIN

You mean Lenin.

LOUIS

That's the dude. Lenin. The point is, he was another ugly motherfucker. Marx, Lenin, all those Russian communist bastards, they're all ugly.

BEN

Marx wasn't Russian and Lenin didn't cause communism in Russia. Corruption and incompetence in the Russian Royal family...//

BRANDON

//...plug it, Ben. You're Humanities. You don't know jack shit. Politics and Economics? What sort of fucking degree is that? You might as well take a degree in Disney cartoons.

(Laughter from Louis and Franklin.)

Look, let's get back to the question here. How are we going to do this?

FRANKLIN

What's the problem? We just get a load of pictures of the ugliest students, print them on flyers and let everyone vote. Or maybe get them to dress up and parade around the quad. What did they do last year?

BRANDON

Flyers are too expensive. Why not just do what they did last year? We ask each of the houses to nominate one guy, then everyone can vote who they think is the ugliest?

LOUIS

Trouble is, who decides who is ugly? What some folk think is ugly, others might not. I mean, look at Ben. Far as I can see, he's one ugly Jewish motherfucker, but I reckon his Momma thinks he's as cute as hell.

(*Everyone except Ben laughs.*)

BEN

At least I have a mother.

(*There is a moments silence. Then Louis jumps up and grabs a handful of Ben's shirt-front.*)

LOUIS

You want to watch that filthy Jew-mouth of yours, man. You need to remember that you're only in this house because your father paid for you to be here. While you're here, you do as we say, you little foreign shit.

(*Louis thrusts Ben away.*)

BRANDON

Hey, Ben! Cut it out. Come on, we got to do this. I get it. None of us gives a shit about charity or whatever, but it's expected. It's part of the price we pay for being...er...//

FRANKIN

//...privileged?

BRANDON

Yeah, well, you might be privileged. Me, I'm just rich as Hell.

(Laughter again, except Ben.)

Look, everyone here knows we've got to do this charity stunt. We don't want to be bagged for failing this...this requirement.

LOUIS

Hey, Ben? No hard feelings, man.

BEN

Would it make any difference?

FRANKLIN

OK, Ben, cut the wounded soldier stuff. We're all in this together, right? Nobody's blaming you for being Jewish, OK? It's unfortunate, but there it is.

BRANDON

OK, so we're going to do this vote.

LOUIS

There's still the matter of what people think they mean by ugly. We could end up with nobody winning. I mean, if we don't get a winner out of this, we're gonna look pretty stupid.

FRANKLIN

That's your problem, Louis baby. You've led too sheltered a life. You don't get people.

BRANDON

Here we go.

FRANKLIN

I've been around politics all my life.

(Brandon speaking in unison with Franklin)

My father was Assistant Governor of Texas for twenty years. You get to know a thing or two about how they vote.

BEN

Who is they?

18

LOUIS

He's talking about the proletariat. The workers. The fucking
Mexicans. Where've you been living, boy?

BRANDON

There're all fucking commies.

FRANKLIN

Thing is, there'll always be a winner. Politics is all about
making sure the winner is who you want to win.

BEN

Like your father.

FRANKLIN

Exactly.

BEN

Or JFK?

FRANKLIN

Hey, screw you, you jerk! He only won because he promised all sorts of shit to your people. You wonder why the Jews have been so mistrusted throughout history? We need a president who'll build a big wall around the country, not just wave in the world's scum.

BEN

How do you think this country came into existence? Virtually everything was built by immigrants. The shipyards, the railways...//

FRANKLIN

//...don't give me all that commie bullshit. This country was built by men like our fathers and grandfathers. They are the real winners here. Not those whingeing civil rights spongers. Look, I've got nothing against the black man, but they have a history of lying and cheating. They can't be trusted. You know what? They're even worse than you Jews!

BEN

My father created one of the biggest banks in California. A trusted company.

FRANKLIN

OK, look, listen up. Just because your father is a multi-millionaire does not make him...it doesn't make him...worthy.

BEN

Just because he is Jewish? It's 1962. Don't you think we should have left all that behind when we defeated the Nazis?

BRANDON

You can't buy your background. You can't deny where you come from.

(*He holds up his hands up in a mock-submissive gesture.*)

I'm not defending the Nazis. What they did was...well, it was definitely wrong. What I mean is, they went about it in the wrong way.

BEN

What, gassing six million people?

LOUIS

What he's saying is, there has to be...order in society. A sort of natural pecking order. The fact is, you people have always tended to...well...undermine that order by hoarding all a country's wealth.

BRANDON

Look...er...Ben. I'm not holding any of this against you. You're a decent dude, man. You don't wear your...your heritage like a coat. You're...quiet about it...which is good.

FRANKLIN

Don't take this personally, Ben. As Brandon said, you're a good guy. You have some...admirable qualities, but the fact remains that society is made of many different levels. It's the way it's always been, man. I mean, think about this. Can you ever imagine a black man as president?

LOUIS

Yeah. Let that sort of thing happen and next you'll be voting for a president who runs a chain of hotels!

BRANDON

OK, Ben, let's cool it. Not get side-tracked...again. Fact is, there will be a winner. We'll make sure of that. The question is, who?

FRANKLIN

Yeah. The democratic process is about giving the people what they need, not what they want. Those civil rights bastards at the Greensbro sit-in need to wake up. Civil rights are about keeping power away from the nut-jobs who would see this great country of ours sink into the shit where everyone is equal. Hell, man, it's history. Once it was about royalty, now it's about the political elite.

BRANDON

We just got rid of divine right, Ben. That's what the revolution was all about. No taxation without representation. Now we vote-in a new administration every four years. But that does not mean just any old motherfucker can get into power. There are mechanisms, processes, selections. You need to get yourself familiar with the way America works, Ben. If you ask me, you spent too many years at that fancy school in Paris.

LOUIS

Can we move on from the history lesson, guys? It's like being in a fucking lecture. I can feel my liver telling me that alcohol is required.

FRANKLIN

Sorry, guys. It just gets my goat when these...these...minorities just reckon that they can muscle in out of some sort of right.

BRANDON

So, we're going with the ugly poll then?

LOUIS

What about that guy...what's his name? Funnel? Frennel? Jesus, that guy is like a...what they call those cavemen?

FRANKLIN

Neanderthals.

LOUIS

Yeah, he's some sort of throw-back.

BEN

His name is Farrell. Lonnie Farrell.

FRANKLIN

Lonnie? What sort of dumb name is that?

LOUIS

So, he qualifies on the basis of having an ugly name as well as being primitive. Perfect!

BRANDON

(*To Ben.*)

You know him? What house is he in?

BEN

We're both members of the Chess Club.

LOUIS

(*Laughing.*)

Well, that's it. Ugly name and a member of the Chess Club,
what could be better?

BEN

I'd just like to say that I'm not happy about...//

FRANKLIN

//...wait a minute! I know this dude. Big guy, greasy hair. Hell!
That dude looks like a pigs backside!

LOUIS

So, you've got personal experience of pigs backsides?

(*Brandon and Louis share a filthy laugh.*)

FRANKLIN

I know they smell better than you do!

BRANDON

OK, OK, let's get a decision made here, can we?

LOUIS

I've got a question.

BRANDON

You've always got a question, Louis. It's a symptom of someone who knows fuck-nothing.

(*Sneering laughter from Franklin and Brandon.*)

LOUIS

I'm serious. What I mean is, why only men?

FRANKLIN

What?

LOUIS

Why confine this poll to men? Why not just get everyone to vote on who is the ugliest man <u>or</u> girl?

BRANDON

I think we can safely lump men and girls together under the little-known noun know as person.

FRANKLIN

Vote for the ugliest person. Doesn't have the same ring about it as vote for the ugliest man. Anyway, are girls ugly? I wouldn't say any of the girls here are ugly. Some of them plain, maybe, but not technically ugly.

LOUIS

Yeah, maybe you're right. Like, if a girl has all the requisite equipment, that makes them attractive in my book.

BRANDON

Can't say I've seen any that don't have all the necessary attributes. Of course, some have more than others.

(*Gestures and snorting sniggers.*)

LOUIS

Yeah, some have more than they can keep safely contained.

(Laughter.)

BEN

And the less attractive ones do give out more readily.

LOUIS

Whoa, Ben! And here was I thinking you were our collective conscience!

FRANKLIN

You know, he's right! The more ugly a girl is, the more likely you'll get inside her panties. You can't deny that.

BRANDON

And how many panties have you been inside, Frank?

LOUIS

But it's an interesting anthropological point. Do the ugly ones put out more easily because they have to compete with the attractive ones, or are they just giving sex to convince themselves that they're not so ugly as they imagine.

BRANDON

Jesus, Louis! Since when has a one-night stand been an
anthropological matter?

BEN

They're always very grateful.

LOUIS

Who are?

BRANDON

Stick with it, Louis. He means the girls, the ugly ones. They're
always grateful if anyone...you know...(*makes an obscene
gesture.*)

LOUIS

Well, I really do think you've redeemed yourself in my eyes,
Ben.

BEN

You just need to tell them that you respect them.

BRANDON

Yeah, right. Not sure that would be enough in your case.

FRANKLIN

You know, one or two of the girls on my course are actually quite intelligent. They always seem to wear glasses through.

LOUIS

Yeah, and underwear made out of titanium. They're not proper girls. They're...un...classified.

LOUIS

So, no girls in the contest.

FRANKLIN

Just ugliest man, then. I'll talk to the other houses. I suggest we get them to nominate candidates. Charge them an entry fee.

BEN

Can I say something?

BRANDON

Is it relevant?

BEN

Don't you think this idea is insulting? Why bother to pick on guys who don't have film-star looks? Would any of you like to be voted as the ugliest man?

(*The other three all bust out laughing.*)

LOUIS

You can't be serious! You're making a proposition that simply cannot be true.

FRANKLIN

Look out, here comes the lawyer.

LOUIS

Bear with me, your Honour. I put it to you, Mr Meitner, that your comment clearly indicates that you're concerned you might end up being voted the winner?

BEN

No! I mean...what I'm saying is...why hold a poll about something so...negative?

LOUIS

Jesus, Ben. You're such a wet wiener sometimes. It's some fun. A laugh.

(*Pause.*)

OK, what do you suggest? A vote on who has the largest prick?

FRANKLIN

Well, he'd lose. Part of his is missing already.

(*Laughter.*)

BEN

I'm just saying. It doesn't seem right to have a laugh at other people's expense.

LOUIS

Christ's sake! Listen to Jesus here. No, wait a minute, you don't believe in Jesus, do you, Ben.

BRANDON

OK, look, I don't think this is going to work if we include both men and girls. Are we agreed that it's about the ugliest man?

(*Franklin and Louis nod and make agreeing noises.*)

BEN

No, I don't want anything to do with this.

BRANDON

Well, that's fine. You can explain to the Dean why you haven't fulfilled your obligation then.

(*Ben stares at the other three for a moment, and then storms off stage.*)

LOUIS

You know what? I've been thinking. Has anyone else seen that girl? The one wearing her Mom's twinset. Weird hair. Fat, and walks like she's got bad haemorrhoids. We should get someone to include her. Now, if she won, that would be totally historic, man.

BRANDON

Yeah. I heard that she sings with some college folk band. Sure-bet she's another of those whingeing civil-rights communists. And serve her right for spoiling the view around here.

LOUIS

Leave it to me. I'll see what I can find out. I'll get someone to nominate her.

FRANKLIN

What if they refuse?

LOUIS

Then I'll nominate her myself.

FADE OUT

SCENE CHANGE TRACK: **Everly Brothers – 'Walk Right Back'**

SCENE 5

FADE UP

BACK PROJECTION

<u>Text</u>: 'November 1966 – Janis' family home, Port Arthur, Texas'
<u>Image</u>: Picture of Janis' family house, Port Arthur.

The family house, Port Arthur, Texas. Janis is stuffing clothes into a suitcase. She is pale,, thin and ill-looking – dark circles under her eyes. Janis' mother, Dorothy, enters.

JANIS

Leave me alone. Just don't bug me.

DOROTHY

Can't we just talk about it? Who's that boy sitting in the car?
Why don't you ask him in?

JANIS

What's the point. Anyway, I ain't staying long. Just grabbing
some clothes. He's a friend.

DOROTHY

Let me say, darlin'...well...your father and I...well...//

JANIS

//...don't say it, Mother. He was a fuckin' shit. OK, I get it.

DOROTHY

Do you have to use words like that? You never used to use profanities.

JANIS

We're talking about how that motherfucker ditched me...my fuckin' fiancé...screwed some other bitch an' got her pregnant an' you're complainin' 'bout my language? Jesus, Mother, get some perspective, will ya?

DOROTHY

I...your father and me...just think it's for the best, that's all.

JANIS

I said. I don't care. I don't know what I was thinkin'. Marriage. That's so straight you could draw lines with it. I don't want straight. I can't be straight. It was...it was a reaction. Tryin' to be someone I'm not.

DOROTHY

It's OK to feel...let down. Disappointed.

JANIS

I ain't disappointed! Look, I'm cool now. That...all that was...stupid. That motherfucker can go bury himself in alimony payments.

DOROTHY

What about...what are you going to do? What about going back...//

JANIS

//...to college? Yeah, yeah. Back into that loving fold. I'm...I'm not going back there. I want to be where people love me. I want to go where people are hip and free of all that shit.

DOROTHY

I know...well...I do know you had some bad times there. I mean, it's the same as life...being a student. It has its good and bad times...like life, I guess. But, I gotta say something...you're looking...er...you look really bad, Jan. I'm...I'm not stupid. I've seen those tracks on your arms. I've seen it on TV. I know what it means. You look ill. Have you been taking drugs?

JANIS

Shit, Mother! Life doesn't have to be about ups and downs. If you're free...if you look for the good stuff and say fuck you to anything and anyone who's pullin' ya down...then...that's what it's gotta be about. Doin' what makes ya happy. Otherwise, what's the point? If you let life be about ups and downs, then...well...then it's gonna be a roller-coaster an' ya might jus' fall off.

DOROTHY

You were always too clever for your own good.

(*Pause.*)

But you had some friends...at college.

JANIS

Don't you get it? I ain't got no friends. Nobody I'd want as a friend anyhow. I'm never gonna find people I wanna be with there, or here. Didn't you read my letter?

DOROTHY

Your letter...well, it was...hard to read. I...I didn't understand what you were sayin' darlin'. Something about a contest at the university? We rang and they said you'd left.

(Janis leaps from the bed.)

JANIS

Jesus, Mother! I...I...I don't know what to say to you! Did you fuckin' read it? I mean...isn't this all your fault? You and Father? I don't know...I mean...why?

DOROTHY

Our fault? What's all our fault? What are you saying, Jan?

JANIS

This, me, everything!

(Janis grabs her cigarettes off the table and lights one.)

DOROTHY

I wish you wouldn't do that, Jan. You know your father doesn't like it.

JANIS

Well, that's just it, isn't it. He smokes his damned pipe, but nobody else is allowed to. I don't get it. He sits down there in *his* chair, drinking *his* whiskey from *his* tumbler, reading *his* paper, listening to fuckin' Mozart and smoking while everyone else has to tippy-toe around. What makes him so special?

DOROTHY

Mind your language! Nothin's gonna get sorted by swearing your head off.

(*Pause. Janis blows a cloud of defiant smoke at the ceiling.*)

Your father...he's the one paying the bills, just you remember that. He works hard. He deserves to have a few things to himself, and, anyway, what's it matter to you? It's about respect. Anyway, he smokes a pipe. It's not proper smoking. He doesn't think a woman smoking cigarettes gives the right...impression.

JANIS

Maybe I should take up smokin' a fuckin' pipe then. And what would that impression be? Someone who is prepared to be nothin' but a domestic slave?

DOROTHY

And you don't know what you're talking about. Since when have you ever been or done anything domestic? Ever since you were ten you've been nothin' but...rebellious. There, I've said it now...//

JANIS

//...rebellious...//

DOROTHY

/...yes! Rebellious is the right word for it. Ask yourself. How many times I got notifications from your high school about your behaviour? And every time we have this discussion, I get the same old story. Oh, sorry, Mother. I didn't mean to cause trouble. It won't happen again.

(*Pause.*)

I blame your grandfather. You've inherited his...difficult streak.

JANIS

What I said in my letter. They went too far. I...I know that I'm a disappointment. To you and Father. But...don't you see...I can't do anything about it. It's me. Anyway...it's your fault I'm like this.

DOROTHY

We didn't understand. What you said in the letter. I didn't understand what you were saying. You know, I rang the university. After I read your letter. Nobody knew where you'd gone.

JANIS

I know, I know. You told me...a number of times. I had to...I just wanted to...I dunno...get away. We've been through this already.

DOROTHY

That contest. They told me you'd nominated yourself. Put your own name into the hat.

JANIS

Yeah, I heard that too.

DOROTHY

You...you never said...if that was true.

JANIS

Jesus, Mother! Look at me. Do you really think I'd fuckin' put my name up for that? Are you serious? That I'd do that...for a laugh? Ask yourself...is that something you'd do to yourself?

DOROTHY

Well...//

JANIS

//...don't bother. Any case. It don't change nothin'. Fact remains that plenty of people there thought I was a serious contender, and, as I said...that's down to you and Father.

DOROTHY

Since you were little, you've always been...strong willed. We've done our level best to teach you how to be...how to be a good person...church...//

JANIS

//...it's not that. It's not what you did or didn't teach me. It's...it's me, the way I am. The way I look. Peter...I...I thought I dug him...that he dug me, but it was a mistake...marriage an' everythin'...I'm...I'm jus' an ugly Texas bitch...//

DOROTHY

//...I...I don't know what you mean. You look just...//

JANIS

//...Mother! For Christ's sake! Just be truthful for once in your life.

(*Pause.*)

OK, OK, look. I'm also not stupid. I know that...you know...bein' a parent...you got to balance out the false from the true. You know. Father Christmas. The fuckin' Tooth Fairy. That sort of stuff. I get it. But...you know...in life...sometimes there are things that can't be denied. The truth of it is there, for everyone to see. You can't do anythin' about it.

DOROTHY

What are you saying? What can't you do anythin' about?

JANIS

Isn't if fuckin' obvious?

(*Dorothy gets up from the chair.*)

DOROTHY

If all you're goin' to do is swear at me, I'm goin' downstairs.

(*Janis goes over to her tote bag and retrieves a copy of the university newspaper. She holds it out to Dorothy.*)

JANIS

This is what you can't do anythin' about.

(*Dorothy unfolds the paper and stares at it. Moments pass as she reads an article there. Finally, she raises a shaking hand to her mouth.*)

DOROTHY

Oh, my God!

JANIS

I'm not goin' back. That's over. Seems like it weren't enough to fuckin' humiliate me. That article is in The Daily Texan- the college's newspaper. Everyone in the State will see it.

DOROTHY

Jan, listen to me. This...it...it doesn't mean anythin'. It's just some ignorant people. Don't let them get to you, darlin', otherwise...otherwise they'll have won.

JANIS

Bein' ignorant don't necessarily make a person wrong.

DOROTHY

Now, you're just twistin' my words. I didn't say they were right. How could I? There are people, in this world, who show their jealousy by hittin' out. Mean people. If you listen to their mean words, then...//

JANIS

//...what? And just what are they jealous of? Exactly what do I have that they don't? Tell me, Mother. What is the basis of their hatred of me? Am I rich? Do I have social influence? Am I powerful? No! I'm an ugly fuckin' working-class girl with no education. Don't...please...don't wrap this up as some sort of jealously. They don't have to be jealous...that's what makes them so...so...oh shit!

DOROTHY

But you do have a talent. Those folk songs you sing. You have a voice, you know that.

JANIS

What, you think these motherfuckers are jealous of me singing? Get real, Mother. Those bastards...the ones who...they wouldn't know singing talent if it were injected up their privileged backsides. They're still listenin' to Frank Sinatra for fuck's sake!

DOROTHY

Well, he is a very good singer. Your father...//

JANIS

//...OK, Mother, this discussion is goin' nowhere. All that stuff, Sinatra, the fuckin' rat pack, it's not real. It's...it's...plastic music. It's, like, moulded on a production line. There's no heart in it. The emotions...they're all manufactured. The stuff I want to sing...it talks about life. Real pain, Mother. Real hurt, real love, real people.

(Pause.)

No, no, I can't do this no more. I've…I've gotta find somethin' that means somethin'. People who mean somethin'. People who don't care how I look…I mean…people who will love me…//

DOROTHY

//…but what are you going to live on? Who's that boy sitting in the car outside? Where are you goin' to stay? Why don't you just take some time? Think about what it is you want. There's no rush.

JANIS

I…I can't live like this. I need to be free. Gotta find out who I am. I know someone. They want me to be in a band. They're called Big Brother and the Holdin' Company. In Frisco. They'll find me a place to stay. I gotta…I got to be true to myself. If you're not bein' true to yourself, then…then, most likely, you're bein' true to someone else. I ain't gonna do that anymore.

(*She picks up her case and heads for the door.*)

I'm sorry. This is jus' the way it's gotta be. That contest. (*Janis points at the paper in her mother's hands.*) The ugliest man on the campus? I didn't win it, but I did come second place. An' that was because the guy who won...he looked like the fuckin' monster from the black lagoon.

(*She pauses in the doorway.*)

Don't worry. I'll write you, OK?

FADEOUT

SCENE CHANGE TRACK: **Janis Joplin- 'Piece Of My Heart'**

SCENE 6

FADE UP – LIGHTS STAGE FRONT LEFT

BACK PROJECTION

Text: 'Recording for a radio station KOLE documentary on Port Arthur's belated honouring of Janis Joplin in 1988.' Image: Any image of Janis relaxing.

Jon is sitting and attaching a lapel microphone as in previous interviews. Again, the audience do not hear the questions posed.

JON

Yeah. Hi, my name's Jon.

What?

I thought we were going to talk about Janis' music. Isn't that what this is all about? Port Arthur saying sorry?

Eh?

What's that got to do with anything? Sure, we were...together. So what? I don't want to talk about that.

Is that right?

Look, plenty has been written about that. Let's just leave it at that. There's nothing I want to contribute. It's all in the past.

What're you getting at?

OK, yeah, I loved her. So did plenty of others.

Special? What's that supposed to mean? What we had was...corrupted...it was destroyed by...//

Eh?

//...yeah, I did love her. Not that she made that easy. We had our differences about...er...lifestyle choices, shall we say.

Right.

OK, we met in Rio. I mean, this is all well-known. You want me to go over all the details again?

Right.

OK, so we had a good time. I didn't know anything about her drug use. She was clean then.

Me?

Yeah, I'm sure. I wasn't a user, but I knew the signs. I'd been around plenty of people who used drugs, so I would have known, you know, if she'd been hiding it.

Real?

Yeah, it was real. She was sweet. Very...into people. She had a kind disposition...naturally. She got people. You know, when we were together in New York, she showed up with this guy in tow. He was just a bum, off the street. A gentle sort, but shit, he really reeked. Jan didn't mind. He needed some help and she gave it, without question. She didn't judge people who she saw were...you know...in need. Sometime after, I thought, well, maybe she just saw someone who was in a worse state than she was. Maybe it made her feel better...that things weren't so bad for her.

Eh?

Er...well, he stole all her clothes, money and booze when we were out one day. But, you know, she took it OK. It was cool that this dude did that. She was OK with it. He was a victim.

You mean how we split?

Sure, she wouldn't compromise. Like, she was into living life for the moment. She was into me in a big way, I knew that, but if you'd asked her about our future together, then...I dunno...you'd get a blank stare I guess. For Janis, thinking about the future was square, straight, know what I mean? Thinking about the future implies responsibility, planning, expectations fulfilled. She wasn't capable of it, and the smack just guillotined that anyway. That's what it does. It makes you focus on the high you've got. The now, the immediate rush, followed by a fog where...I dunno...reality has been erased.

Right.

Yeah, I know she got clean...later. But I'd moved on. I couldn't handle seeing her like that. It was killing her, slowly, like some weird weed killer. You don't see the effects right away, but you know it's eating away inside. We argued about it. I had to go.

Eh?

I don't know what that means. What's that supposed to mean, 'enabler'?

Is that right?

Well, let me tell you something, Mister. I did everything in my power to get her to stop, short of locking her up in a cage.

(*Getting upset.*)

You people...you've no right to go using terms like that...no right at all. Unless you've lived with an addict. An' it don't matter what. Booze...smack...uppers...downers...it don't make no difference.

(Jon rubs his face. He begins to break down.)

Look...I should never have left her. I know that now. She needed me...and...I was...weak. Selfish. I couldn't control it. The dope. I was used to...you know...being in control. In life. But, it beat me. The smack she took. I was collateral damage.

(Tearful...)

Don't you think...after all this time...that I don't regret...I...I sent her a telegram. From Kathmandu. You any idea how hard that is? I knew...

(Angry.)

She should have got that telegram. Someone screwed up. That fucking hotel. I sensed it. I knew...

...we could've been...

(Scene change track starts low volume. He puts his head in his hands and says, almost to himself...)

...every junkie's like a setting sun.

FADEOUT

SCENE CHANGE TRACK: **Neil Young – 'The Needle and the Damage Done'**

SCENE 7

FADEUP

BACK PROJECTION:

Text: 'September 14, 1968 – Fillmore West concert.'
Image: Any on-stage picture of Janis.

There is the gradually fading background sound of an audience cheering, etc. as Janis enters her changing room alone at the Fillmore West, a bottle of Southern Comfort swinging from her fingertips. After taking a swig, she collapses onto a couch and fumbles for a cigarette and lighter off the dressing table.

After a few moments, Janis struggles to her feet and approaches a full-length mirror at stage front (as before). She removes the ostrich feathers from her hair and then pulls contorted faces at her reflection.

JANIS

Jesus fucking H Christ!

(Turning away in disgust and then spinning around to confront the image, or is it the audience? Pointing...)

What the fuck are you looking at? Ain't you seen a walking dead person before. What's that word...er...shit...the fucking walking dead...zombies! Fucking zombie.

(Striding away from the mirror, but then returning...)

You know somethin'? I was born dead. Yeah. When I popped out of my mother, nurse thought I was good an' dead. Got a good old Texas smack on my ass. Enough to resurrect Jesus, an' no mistake. But, you know what. I tricked 'em. I was dead then, an' I stayed dead. I'm a singing zombie, man. I only come alive when I sing. That means one thing. Here...now...you an' me - we're both dead.

(There is a knock on the door. Janis hastily grabs the ostrich feathers from the floor and re-applies them to her hair.)

Go the fuck away!

(The door opens gingerly and a man's head appears. The audience recognise him as one of the frat brats who named Janis as The Ugliest Man. Janis, however, does not know him. He is dressed in a conventional, conservative 1960s style ie sports jacket and slacks.)

LOUIS

Hi! OK, if I come in?

JANIS

I dunno. Who are you? What'ya doin' here, man?

LOUIS

Oh, er, well, I came to see you. The show, I mean. You might say we've got a sort of connection.

(*He steps into the room.*)

JANIS

An' did ya like it? The show?

LOUIS

Sure, sure.

JANIS

You ain't soundin' so sure to me, man, an' you certainly ain't dressed like anyone else in that audience.

(*Louis looks himself over.*)

Anyway, I meant, what're you doin' back here, back stage? How'd you get past my 'vicious guard dogs'?

LOUIS

Didn't see any guard dogs. There was a guy. I told him who I was and he said it would be OK.

JANIS

Oh, he fuckin' did, did he?

(*Pause. Louis gesticulates as if he's trying to broach a difficult subject.*)

You wanna drink? (*Janis holds up the bottle.*)

LOUIS

Er...no, I'm OK.

JANIS

Cheers!

(*Janis takes a swig from the bottle.*)
So, who are you, man?

LOUIS

What?

JANIS

What the hell, man? You said you told the guy outside, my vicious guard dog, who you were. That suggests that you are somebody, man. So, who are you? You looking to ball me, or what?

LOUIS

Right. Yeah. Er...no. Name's Louis.

(*He holds out his hand.*)

JANIS

(*Ignoring the offered hand...*)

OK, Mr Louis, it's been very nice to meet you, but I'm afraid that to be somebody, you need more than just bein' called Louis. Anyway, I'm not going to ball you. You're not my type.

LOUIS

Er...yeah...of course...no...what I mean is, I'm Louis...from your old college. Austin. I was there when you were...well, briefly, back in 65.

(There is a long pause. The bottle falls from Janis' fingers and clatters to the floor.)

JANIS

University of Texas? You were there, man?

LOUIS

S'right.

JANIS

Right. OK. Sixty-five. Yeah. I fuckin' remember that, man. Don't rightly remember you though. What do ya want? They finally decided to award my honorary degree?

LOUIS

Er, no, and we didn't actually meet. I was Alpha Phi Omega.

JANIS

Right. One of those privileged motherfuckers.

LOUIS

Well, I don't know about privileged.

JANIS

So, tell me, Mr fuckin' Privileged Motherfucker Louis, how come an Alpha Phi Omega noticed a nobody Texas country girl like me?

LOUIS

OK, well, obviously, everyone knew who you were.

JANIS

Everyone at college knew who I was. Is that right? Can't say that I fuckin' noticed people waving and sayin' 'Hi Janis, howya doin''. How d'ya explain that, Mr Rich-boy Louis?

LOUIS

Er...right...well...there was your music, of course. The folk band.

JANIS

And did you, or any of your Alpha Phi Omega friends come to see me...in the folk band?

63

LOUIS

Um...no...not rightly. We knew of it...the band...//

JANIS

//...you recall the name of this band?

LOUIS

Um...not rightly. It's...er...it's slipped...//

JANIS

//...and how did you come to know of a band that you an' ya
friends had no intention of seein' perform and can't
remember the fuckin' name of?

LOUIS

Hey! Look...let's not get hung up on all that old stuff. It's in the
past. We've all moved on, right?

JANIS

Fuckin' moved on from what, man? Like a body moves away
from a pile of stinkin' shit, you mean?

LOUIS

You know, that whole...misunderstanding...//

JANIS

//...misunderstanding? The only misunderstanding I had was that college was supposed to be a place for free-thinkers. Turned out it was a place for people who didn't think at all.

LOUIS

Er...yeah. No. I mean...that competition.

(Janis realises what Louis is referring to. To have this most painful of memories suddenly brought out into the open by a complete stranger catches her off-guard. Louis watches as Janis freezes, lost in some personal agony once again. After a while, she says...)

JANIS

What...do you know...about that, man? Why are you draggin' that up?

LOUIS

OK, look...Janis...you mind if I call you Janis?

65

JANIS

I've just become Miss Joplin to you, man.

LOUIS

Right. Well, you know, I came here, tonight. I saw the advertising...for your concert. I work near here. Anyways, I thought...I thought...well, I thought I should apologise.

JANIS

You...you came here...to apologise?

LOUIS

Yeah. Yeah, I did. I felt...you know...well...I felt, now that you're famous...well...I should say that I'm sorry...for any hurt I might have caused.

JANIS

Hurt? Apologise for any hurt? Now that I'm famous?

LOUIS

Sure. I mean, it was just a stupid stunt. It had been done before. Previous years. Sort of tradition. I had no idea...

(Pause.)

JANIS

You...you had no idea.

LOUIS

Right. It was just a dumb thing. You know. Everyone does stupid things when they're at college. You know...it's...it's...expected.

JANIS

OK, Mr Whatever your name is, let me get my head around this. You're sayin' that you had something to do with that fuckin' contest? An involvement?

LOUIS

Not Involvement? Actually...the college wanted to...you know...ban it. But we thought...where's the harm? That's why I'm here...to say...//

JANIS

//...that fucking contest was your idea?

LOUIS

Right. Er no, not my idea, but look...

JANIS

You know whose idea it was to nominate me?

LOUIS

OK...look, this is getting out of hand. I came here to offer...//

JANIS

//...yeah, you already said that. To apologise. So, who are you apologising for? You? Or somebody else?

LOUIS

(*There is a moment where Louis is speechless. He points at Janis.*)

Right. Stop right there! Let's get something clear little Miss Hippy. I didn't need to come here tonight, but I'm a gentleman. When I offend, I admit it and offer my hand. But, you know what...that contest, The Ugliest Man on Campus? Get this into your stupid hippy female head...it was no big deal. And I'll let you into another useful fact. The contest? No, not my idea, but tracking you down and nominating you...that was me.

(Janis slowly sinks to the floor, draws her knees up and curls into a tight ball.)

And here's another bit of advice. Don't go getting the idea that because you can stir up those poor deluded kids out there, that this justifies any sort of respect. I mean, take a fucking close look at yourself. You dress and smell like some wino.

(Aware that he might have gone too far...)

Look...I think you're making too big a thing over this. For Christ's sake! It was just a college stunt. A bit of fun. Nobody took it seriously, I mean, after all...you sort of asked for it...really...all that weirdness. Nobody understood what you were saying for Christ's sake! One day you're dressed like an undertaker, next like your grandmother. Now I came here to make it clear that I don't hold any of this against you. I get it. You're a woman. I understand. But I wanted to offer my hand...like a gentleman.

(Janis suddenly uncoils like a released spring and lets out a chilling scream. She lobs the bottle at Louis, narrowly missing him.)

Hey! Whoa now...//

JANIS

(*Shouting.*)

//...you...responsible for that...that...//

LOUIS

//...hey, hey! I said...take it easy.

(*Janis suddenly launches herself at Louis and grabs his throat in both hands. They struggle, locked together, crashing into furniture, etc. After a few minutes of desperate tussle, the door opens and a startled stage hand enters. He finally separates Janis from Louis who, shocked and rubbing his throat, beats a hasty retreat. Janis sinks to the floor, inconsolable.*)

FADEOUT

SCENE CHANGE MUSIC: The Kinks – 'I'm Not Like Everybody Else'

SCENE 8

FADEUP

BACK PROJECTION:

<u>Text</u>: 'September 1969 - Legal Offices of Janis' Lawyer'
<u>Image</u>: Any picture of Janis wearing her feathers.

Janis is standing in her lawyer's office, bottle of Southern Comfort hanging from her fingers once again. Seated behind the desk is a smart, suited lawyer. He removes his glasses and speaks...

ROBERT

You're fucking drunk.

JANIS

I don't get drunk. You should know that by now. This (*holds up bottle*), this is what keeps me sane, man. This keeps me sober.

ROBERT

It might keep you sane, but it also keeps getting you into trouble. That, and other stuff.

71

JANIS

This about that fuckin' TV commercial? I thought you were dealin' with that. I'm tellin' you, Bob, I want the balls of the guy runnin' that agency served up with hot chilli sauce. Ain't nobody gonna use me without my say so. If I'm gonna be used...I like to know about it.

BOB

That's being dealt with. This is something else, Jan.

JANIS

Yeah, well, that's what I pay you for, Robert. To make the fuckin' trouble go away.

ROBERT

Sit down, Janis...please.

JANIS

(Janis jumps up on the chair facing the desk.)

Sit, sit, sit. Sit is shit, man. Sit down an' be controlled. Let me tell you somethin'. My concerts...the one's that got cancelled by those motherfuckers, you know the ones, jus' because they wouldn't let 'em out of their seats. No dancing. Stay in ya seat an' be quiet. Jesus, man! This is one of my gigs. How are people supposed to get loose, man. I mean...fucking stay in ya seat or we'll arrest you. What the fuck's that about?

ROBERT

You know what it's about Janis.

JANIS

Fuckin' repression. That's what it's about. Kids...they jus' wanna have some fun...//

ROBERT

//...I know all this. I have to draw up your contracts, remember?

JANIS

Yeah, an' what do we have here. (*Picks up a paper from the desk.*) I have to...promise...no, guarantee, that my audiences...my people...people who love me...I have to make them stay in their seats! What the fuck, Bob?

ROBERT

It's just a clause to keep the venues happy. You know this, Janis. Why are we going over all this again. All you have to do is stop the kids ripping the place apart. So long as there's no damage...

JANIS

Damage? What fuckin' damage, man? I ain't ever heard tell of any damage done at my gigs...//

ROBERT

//...I know, I know. It's the potential, Janis. People, the great white American public...they're scared of those kids. Scared that they're out of control. That you make them out of control.

JANIS

I make 'em happy! Jesus! Where's the fuckin' crime in bein' happy, Bob?

ROBERT

OK, Janis...we've had this debate a few times. You get drunk and you kick back. But I'm not your enemy, J J. I'm on your side, but we have to play by the rules...otherwise...well, things could get bad for you. And this is why you're here today. We've got to deal with this. Cut it down before it grows too big. You understand?

(*Janis curls up in the chair like a child, hugging the bottle.*)

This...accusation...(*Robert waves a letter*), they're threatening prosecution...lodging a complaint against you, Janis. Do you get that?

JANIS

I don't give a shit. That motherfucker...he...he...I don't wanna talk about it.

ROBERT

He claims that he came to see you after a concert and that you suddenly went berserk and attacked him. Says that one of your roadies had to pull you off.

(*Pause. Janis swigs from the bottle. It is now empty. She carefully places it on Robert's desk.*)

Jesus Christ, Janis! I'm asking if this is true!

JANIS

(Sitting upright.)

Who gives a shit? Anyway, I don't want to talk about it. Far as I'm concerned...got what he had comin'.

ROBERT

Did he try it on? Force himself on you, something like that. If he did, we could argue self-defence. If they decide to go to court.

JANIS

(Almost inaudibly...)

No.

ROBERT

What?

JANIS

(Shouting.) No! What the fuck, Bob?

ROBERT

So, you did assault this guy. Just tell me why, Janis. Maybe there <u>was</u> no reason. Had you been using?

JANIS

No! Not that.

ROBERT

What then?

JANIS

For fuck's sake , Bob. Can't you just leave it. Tell this motherfucker and his lawyer to go screw 'emselves. Ain't that what you lawyers do?

ROBERT

Don't think that's gonna work in this case, Janis. The motherfucker's lawyers, as you put it, are an old LA firm. Big money. Someone's funding this and I reckon they're not going away until they get what they want.

JANIS

So, what do they want, man? Jus give it to 'em for fuck's sake.

ROBERT

Why'd you attack him, Janis?

(Pause. Janis hides her face in her hands.)

Need to know, babe. The truth. Then...well...I'll see what I can do...//

JANIS

(Janis suddenly stands and storms off around the room, pulling her hair and kicking a small table over. Shouting, she says...)

//...I'm so fuckin' done with this...Jesus! My whole fuckin' life. Why can't people jus' let me be free? Everything...everything I've done I've had to deal with other people's shit. What to say, what to wear, how to fuckin' behave. I'm...I'm...I'm a jigsaw...yeah a jigsaw. Pieces...everyone putting a piece here, piece there...tryin' to make a picture of what they want me to be.

(She sinks to her knees in tears.)

The only place...I can be...me...is up there. On stage. It's the only time nobody's buggin me, man. I call the shots. I do what I want. Yeah, I get them up on their seats and fuck anybody who says no!

(*Pause. Her anger subsides.*)

Thing is, Bob. I ain't doin' anythin' wrong, man. I'm just singin' an' givin' people some hope. Some light. What's so wrong in that? All I want is to be...loved.

(*Long pause.*)

ROBERT

Right.

(*Pause.*)

OK. I'll see what I can do. Gotta feeling that this guy is after some sort of payment. Maybe if we offered some...compensation.

JANIS

Give that fuck-face money?

ROBERT

You said it. Give them what they want. If you won't tell me what this is all about, then my options are limited. If it goes to court and they subpoena that stagehand...well...

JANIS

That piece of dog shit ruins my life an' he gets paid for it?

ROBERT

Tell me what he did and we'll see.

JANIS

OK. OK. I'll tell you. I'll say what that shit-filled scumbag did. He was born a man, that's what. A man, like all the other motherfuckers, who think a woman is nothin' more than a place to park their dicks. You want to know what he did to me? He made me understand somethin'...he made me understand that if beauty is skin-deep, ugly goes clean to the fuckin' bone.

(Janis fiddles in her tote bag an pulls out a half-empty quart of Southern Comfort. She takes a swig.)

80

ROBERT

All this is telling me is that you've got a downer on men today. What happen? Some pretty boy turn you down last night?

JANIS

(Janis gets up and moves around the desk to Bob's side.)

Here, enjoy a bit of southern discomfort, you patronizin' shit.

(She empties the remainder of the Southern Comfort bottle over his head then slams the bottle down on the desk.)

Now, you an' me, we've been friends sometime now, but don't you go mistakin' friendship for ownership. Nobody fucking owns me, an' that gives me the right to ball whoever I want, right?

ROBERT

Whomever...it's whomever you want.

JANIS

Whomever, whoever, they're still the same dick on a stick with sprinkles.

ROBERT

Why put yourself down like this, J J? You're worth a thousand of those dudes. They're just using you.

JANIS

(Janis climbs onto Robert's desk.)

Goddam right. They're using me because all I've got to offer is what I got right here. *(She points to her crotch.)* As I said, ugly goes clean to the bone an' there ain't nothin' I can do about it.

(She picks up one of the empty bottles and stares at it.)

You wanna know what that guy an' his friends did to me? I'll tell you, man. He proved to me that, bitches like me...we're never gonna get on the cover of Vogue, an' you know why? Because women want it...that appreciation by men...too much, an' that's our weakness. Every woman's magazine is fuckin' edited by a woman for Christ's sake! Take a moment to think why that is, man. For that reason...we'll never inherit the earth.

FADEOUT

SCENE CHANGE MUSIC: Steppenwolf – 'Born To Be Wild'

SCENE 9

FADE UP – LIGHTS STAGE FRONT RIGHT

BACK PROJECTION:

<u>Text</u>: **March, 1970 – Janis' house 'Larkspur'**
<u>Image</u>: **Picture of 'Larkspur'.**

Janis' Larkspur house after her return from Rio. She has been using heroin again making her mood alternate between languid and dangerous. Jon has been attempting to get Janis to stop using. Janis is sprawled on the sofa taking regular swigs from a bottle of Southern Comfort throughout the scene. Jon is standing with is back to her, stage front.

JANIS

Come on, Baby. Chill why don't ya? What's ya problem?

JON

I don't get it. I just don't get why you're doing this to yourself. You're fucking killing yourself for...what? Some stupid fake hippy dream about living in the moment? In Rio...//

JANIS

//...fuck Rio! That was then. This is now, man.

(Janis curls up and becomes morose.)

I'm...I'm sorry, baby. I'll do it. Yeah, I'll kick this motherfucker. I really mean it. Do you love me?

JON

You said that. When I got back. I've been here two weeks watching you shoot up an' every time, it's; I'll kick this, baby...I don't need it...just give me some time. It's bullshit, man. You've got to want to stop more than you want to go on. I just don't see it.

JANIS

But everyone loves me. I'm a star an' everyone fuckin' loves me...don't they? Do you love me?

JON

Of course.

JANIS

You really love me?

JON

I just said...//

JANIS

//...yeah, but do you <u>love</u> me? You know...real love.

JON

You know I do, but, you've got to get real, babe. These people...they don't love you. They're fucking using you. Dudes show up here an' nobody knows who they are. They crash and eat your food, drink your booze, sleep anywhere they pass out. It's all happening while your strung out Babe. There's no control.

JANIS

Fuck control! I don't want to fuckin' live under anyone's control. That ain't real, that's for suckers, man. Like those motherfuckers back there, in Port Arthur. They're hooked on control. It's a drug. It's worse than smack, man. I can give that up...anytime I want. Can they? Can those motherfuckers give up controlling each other?

JON

You're talking crap, Janis. I don't care about them, Port Arthur, whatever. This is about us, babe. You an' me. I can't watch you destroy yourself. You keep staying you wanna quit. You're never gonna be out of this shit while you're swimming in it. Nobody's sayin' that you have to give up singing...not forever. But this...it's...there's no future...//

JANIS

//...don't throw that fucking future shit at me!

JON

Why not? If there's no future, then there's no future for us, man. I love you. You're the most...the most, fucking amazing person I've ever met. I want a future with you.

JANIS

An' I do too, Baby. I wanna give it up. Soon, when I'm really a star.

JON

What do you mean...a star? You're the most recognisable woman in the world. What more do you want?

JANIS

I just want them to love me, Baby.

JON

Who? Who you want to love you?

JANIS

Everyone.

JON

But I'm not everyone, Babe. I'm the opposite of everyone. I'm someone. I can't do this. I'm going back on the road. I want you there. I want you to see what I see. Be part of it.

JANIS

Well, why don't you just fuck off then? Fuck right out, man. You say you love me...but...it's a...it's pussy-love. If you really love a body, then...then, you'll do whatever it takes to stay.

This is me. It's who I fuckin' am. Who cares! I can ball a cat every night. More than one. I've balled a thousand men before you. Any time I want. That's why they do it...'cos they love me. They want a piece of Janis Joplin an' I give it 'em. Go screw some chick in Kathmandu. Screw a hundred.

JON

Don't do this, Janis. Don't fabricate yourself. You want real? Then look in your heart. Shooting smack isn't real, man. It's a fantasy.

JANIS

It's all fuckin' fantasy, man. You, me, them. Life is one big fucking pantomime. Only for me, it's...it's...I'm everybody's ugly sister. Nobody is looking at me an' sayin', shit man, she should marry Prince Charming. I'm an ugly chick an' all I've got is what I have. My voice. A...a...diamond trapped in a shithole.

(They stare at each other.)

I can't stand it!

(Pause.)

No...wait...I love it! It's the biggest buzz, man. To be an ugly chick, and then to ball anybody I want because I'm a fuckin' star. Those chicks. At my gigs. They get balled because they're pretty. You know what? That's not real, man. Real is being able to reach into cats' hearts and rip 'em out just by singing...and then I ball 'em.

JON

So, I'm just some random screw? Some pretty boy you picked up in Rio?

JANIS

If that's how you wanna see it.

JON

You love me. I know it. So, why are you throwing this all away? Isn't what we have worth kicking smack for? Cutting down on the booze? Letting the real you, the one I found in Rio, out of the cage you've locked yourself in?

JANIS

Yeah, but I didn't make this cage. I'm an animal. They put me in this cage, man. Back then. They said, It's ugly, we don't get it, quick, trap it in this cage, shut the door and throw away the key.

JON

This...it's all in your imagination...this...thing...about being ugly.
I don't think you're ugly, the boys in the band don't think
you're ugly. Your record label doesn't think you're ugly...///

JANIS

Yeah, yeah...I've heard it all before, man. But, the thing is,
it's...it's like the emperor's clothes. When I was nobody, all I
got were the sneers an' the pointin' fingers. Now I'm
somebody, those fingers ain't pointin' anymore. They're too
busy being fingers in my pie, man. That's the truth of it...//

JON

//...well, you know what? I'm in agreement there. You've got
so many fingers in your pie that there's no room for anything
else...including me!

JANIS

You don't get it because you're a fuckin' man. You don't know
what it feels like to exist below the required standard. Ugly?
That's a relative term, man, but it IS a term that gets applied
by other people. It's a label, like bein' black, or crippled, or any
other thing that makes you different. That's why I had to leave
Port Arthur...because they made bein' the same a virtue, like

Jesus somehow said that the identical shall inherit the earth. But, you know what? He was fuckin' right. It IS the conformists who'll inherit the earth because they're all weak. The strong don't fuckin' want the earth, man! The weak are the same as the strong because they don't have the strength to be different. They don't believe in themselves enough to live life the way they want to, so they live life the way everyone else wants 'em to.

JON

Being different doesn't make you ugly. And if all this is everyone else's shit...why let it bother you?

JANIS

Because bein' ugly... it means that you can't be loved, man. Some guy...he can ball you in the evenin', but come mornin', all he sees is some ugly bitch. Love never gets the chance to grow.

JON

This is all bullshit!

JANIS

Bein' ugly may be other people's judgement of me, but if it stops me bein' loved...then I might as well make it my own.

(Jon moves to leave while Janis reaches out a hand to him.)

Don't leave me, baby!

JON

(Jon reaches out to Janis.)

Come with me.

JANIS

I...I can't. Please...stay...stay with me, baby.

FADEOUT

SCENE CHANGE MUSIC: The Shirelles-'Will You Still Love Me Tomorrow'

SCENE 10

FADE UP – LIGHTS STAGE FRONT LEFT

BACK PROJECTION:

<u>Text:</u> 'Recording for a radio station KOLE documentary on Port Arthur's belated honouring of Janis Joplin in 1988.'
<u>Image:</u> Any image of Janis and Peggy Casserta

Pearl is sitting and attaching a lapel microphone as in previous interviews. Again, the audience do not hear the questions posed.

PEARL

You know I wrote a book about all this?

What?

Oh, right. OK. Er...Well, I'm Pearl. Janis and me, well, we were good friends back then. As I was sayin', I put all this stuff in my book.

Are you serious?

OK, so I had some help, so what? I don't want to talk about that bastard. Fact is, most of what I had to say is in there somewheres. You know, I don't really get why her home town is doin' all this self-recrimination shit. Fact is, if anyone was to blame for her passing, it was them. Don't think they'll be putting their hand up to that.

Eh?

Yeah, Janis and me were close, you could say that. We had our moments. Nobody'd pass comment on it now, but back then it was...I dunno...part of the scene and not part of the scene, if you get me.

What do I mean?

Well, I suppose I mean that, you know, girls having an affair was sort of seen as being free, in those circles anyway. I'm not ashamed of it.

No.

OK, so, I guess...what I'm trying to say is, it was accepted but not talked about.

No, not long. Couple of months, I suppose.

Right. Do we have to talk about her death. I mean, what's to say?

Not sure I want to go over all that, even after all these years.

Is that right?

Yes, I was supposed to be with her on that Friday. It's a matter of record.

Is this fuckin' relevant?

Why are you dragging this up? There are a thousand websites claiming I abandoned her. She killed herself because I wasn't there for her, blah, blah, blah. Can you imagine what it's been like living with that accusation for fifty years?

Look, I agreed to this 'cos I thought we were going to talk about her music.

No, of course I don't agree. I rang the hotel that Saturday night. They told me she'd asked not to be disturbed. You know this.

Pissed? Yeah, I was pissed about that. Look, Janis...she could be...you know...petty...vindictive. She'd blocked my calls because I'd let her down on that Friday. Sure, maybe I should have called, but it wasn't like that...back then. There weren't any mobile phones. Arrangements were...loose. For fuck's sake, you can't rely on people who are taking drugs...including me!

Tragic? I'll tell you something...I've never said this before.

(*Pause.*)

Janis lived her whole life in pain, well certainly from about 15 onwards. She was just some scrawny kid before, but when those hormones kicked in, they ate her alive, man. Overnight, her skin went...well, you know all this, right? By the time she was 15, well, the fact was, she was not a conventional good-looker. I saw her. Sometimes, well she was scary. She could look so bad. Everyone put the puffy, yellow skin down to booze and drugs. It wasn't, an' that's a fact. There were days when she just looked terrible...and she knew it. All those ostrich feathers? They were a barrier she got hooked on. Got to the point where she wouldn't see anybody without them. Even me sometimes. And the worst of it was, she knew what everyone was thinking, or thought she did. All those years. And nobody ever said. None of the guys in any of the bands. But the boys she picked up screwed her because she offered it on a plate, not because they were captivated by her stunning looks.

What?

Listen! I was like everyone else. But I was her friend. More of a friend than most. Yeah, we were all fucked up by the smack. Sure, it was a bad time, but I never forced her to do it. When she was clean, I stayed away...mostly. No, I never said to her, Hey babe, maybe you need to rethink how you see yourself. I'll admit it, like everyone else, we were all on the bandwagon. Having a good time. Living life. Janis encouraged that...most of the time.

Me? Responsible?

(*Getting upset.*)

OK, smart-ass. You misrepresented what this was all gonna be about. But, let me tell you straight. Janis died because she was tired of being lonely and that's a fact. Of having nobody she could love. Jon was the only one who truly loved her for what she was. He wasn't interested in her music. He came to her in Rio as just this...I dunno...intelligent, caring...I mean, he was a school teacher for Christ's sake! Not someone looking to exploit her. They were soul-mates. But you know what? She chased him away because she just could not believe that he could love an ugly bitch like her. She was so damaged by the whole world's perception of her appearance that she couldn't even see true love when she had it in the palm of her hand. That's the real tragedy. She was a simple girl who paid the price for not behaving like a housewife. You know what? The world is still full of ugly housewives. If you want to break those shackles, every woman on a magazine cover, every TV weather girl, every female TV presenter means you gotta look something special, otherwise you're just gonna attract a load of hate and loneliness, an' not just from men. It was true then and it's still true today.

What?

Well, you're a man. What the fuck do you know?

FADEOUT

SCENE CHANGE MUSIC: The Who – 'I'm A Man'

SCENE 11

FADEUP

BACK PROJECTION:

<u>Text</u>: 'August 1970 -Janis' manager, Albert B. Grossman's office'
<u>Image</u>: Picture of A B Grossman and Janis.

Scene opens with Albert sitting relaxed behind a business desk. John Cooke, Janis' road manager, is standing accusingly, pointing his finger at Albert.

COOKE

You're the one who gave me this job, for Christ's sake! Pulled me out of a band to be her wet-nurse...//

GROSSMAN

//...I gave you a fucking job, John, when that band of yours was dead in the water.

(*Pause. Cooke turns his back on Grossman.*)

Look...you get a call from some dead-beat singer-song writer. So what?

COOKE

Jesus, Al. Why do you have to be so down on everyone. Toby's a fine writer, and in any case, I trust him. If he's saying that Janis is going to die...well...I reckon we should...maybe...pay attention, that's all.

GROSSMAN

Don't you say that! I don't wanna hear you saying that. She's OK. We've been here before. The smack, I challenged her and she quit. Same with the speed. She's got balls and don't you forget it. She won't jeopardise her career.

COOKE

When was the last time you went to see her, Al?

(*Grossman raises his hands and shrugs.*)

Exactly. You weren't there, Al. At El Quijote. Even I noticed it, man. She was pink. It was weird. Backstage...I'm telling you, it was like she had bad sunburn. She needs help.

GROSSMAN

Pink. You're saying she's gonna die because she was a bit flushed in the face?

COOKE

This guy, Toby, he was really scared. Maybe he knows something we don't. It chilled me, Al, the way he spoke about her, like maybe he'd seen something like it before, I don't know. I think you need to talk to him.

GROSSMAN

Let me ask you, John. You're her road manager, right? So what have you done to keep her clean? And I don't just mean the drugs, I'm talking booze as well.

COOKE

Hey! No, no, no. You're not going to lay that at my door. You know what it's like. Every place, every hotel, every venue, there's someone offering stuff. In any case, trying to tell Janis what she can and can't do is asking for trouble. It's a delicate balance. She's off the smack. The booze...well that's a whole different issue.

GROSSMAN

And what do you suggest I do, John? You said it yourself, giving her instructions is likely to get your balls unscrewed, cooked and served up in tomato sauce. And you know what? Since her success, she's gotten more difficult...by a big margin.

(Pause.)

I was relying on you, John...to keep a lid on things.

COOKE

It's impossible, Al. You don't see it. There's something about
her...something...I don't know...corrosive. Something eating
away at her.

GROSSMAN

You think it might be about her high school? That visit. I heard
you went with her. Maybe her going back was a bad idea. She
wanted to go back to kick some ass. I told her not to go.

COOKE

Yeah, can't say I was too happy about it. Reunions? People go
there wanting to see how old friends have changed and all
they find is that those people haven't changed at all and they
weren't ever friends either.

GROSSMAN

You're right. You discover that the only good thing about the past is that it's in the past. Dig up a load of old ghosts and all you're gonna get are dirty hands.

COOKE

Not sure you can dig up ghosts...anyway, it proved to be a bad idea. Something happened at the Pelican Club at Port Arthur. Jerry Lee Lewis being a complete shit, I mean.

GROSSMAN

You see that?

COOKE

No. I was told that she went backstage to Jerry's dressing room. You know he'd refused to see her at a previous gig?

GROSSMAN

Yeah, I'd heard that. I was told that he hated Janis. For my money, I reckon he couldn't handle the fact that a woman had become so successful. Let's not forget, he is a southern gentleman.

(Pause.)

So, what happened? Was she looking for trouble?

COOKE

From what I heard, the opposite. She went to congratulate him on a great performance.

GROSSMAN

So...what? Never heard that Jerry ever objected to being told he was great.

COOKE

No, definitely not. The trouble started when Janis introduced her sister to him.

(Pause.)

GROSSMAN

And?

COOKE

Turns out Jerry made some inappropriate comment. Janis took exception and took a swing at him. Jerry hit back. Couple of Jerry's people had to escort Janis out of the room.

GROSSMAN

Jesus! What the hell did he say? Must have been something bad for Janis to get violent. Most times, she'd have just given him a few Texas verbs.

COOKE

Yeah, well, from what I hear, it wasn't the most gentlemanly thing to say.

GROSSMAN

(*Pause.*)

Christ, John, you waiting for a writer's fee or something?

COOKE

OK, so, when Janis introduces her sister, Jerry says to Janis' sister, Laura, something like, 'You wouldn't be bad looking if you weren't trying to look like your sister'.

GROSSMAN

Jesus, what an ass!

COOKE

Right. Definitely pushed a button for Janis. As you say, the violence was accompanied by plenty of invective, on both parts.

GROSSMAN

Right. Nobody deemed it appropriate to tell me about this...//

COOKE

//...well there's plenty that people don't tell you about, Al. That's what I'm getting at. There's stuff going on...in her head...that you don't know about. Look, we all get carried away. The booze, a bit of candy here and there, and I know you don't approve, but for what it's worth, her booze consumption is not about feeling good, it's about not feeling bad. There's a big difference, Al.

GROSSMAN

As I said, John. She's stronger than you think.

COOKE

If you'd seen her at El Quijote, you'd think different. Far as I can see, Toby's got a point. I told him that the situation was complicated and he came right back with a denial. He said that it wasn't complicated. The fact is, according to him, Janis has no real friends. The sort that are prepared to step up and tell her like it is.

GROSSMAN

What does he know? How long has he known her?

COOKE

That's not the point.

GROSSMAN

What is your point.

COOKE

I...I don't know. Maybe we should look at her schedule. Try to get her to take some time away...a different country...somewhere clean. What's that country where booze is illegal?

GROSSMAN

You think that's going to deal with the demons in her head;
pack her off to a desert?

COOKE

Maybe not, but it might just keep her from killing herself.

GROSSMAN

Yeah, but would she still be the greatest blues singer in
history?

FADEOUT

SCENE CHANGE MUSIC: Bessie Smith – 'Wasted Life Blues'

SCENE 12

SLOW FADEUP

BACK PROJECTION:

<u>Text</u>: 'Landmark Hotel, October 4, 1970'
<u>Image</u>: Picture of the Landmark Hotel

SOUND: Audio from one of Janis' concerts (song: 'Maybe'), including her banter with audience.

Janis' Motel room at the Landmark Hotel. At lights up, Janis is lying face down on the floor between the bed and a bedside table. She is wearing a nightie. This scene has no dialogue and is acted out against a soundscape of one of her live performances. The door is broken down and John Cooke staggers in. He sees Janis on the floor and races to check her out. He is distraught. After a few minutes, he uses the phone. Minutes later Robert, Janis' lawyer, arrives. There is a shared emotional moment between John and Robert. Robert proceeds to search the bed, bedside cabinet, etc. looking for incriminating evidence of drug use. He finds nothing.
The scene closes with John Cooke scooping up Janis' dead body and cradling her in his arms as he sobs, sitting on the edge of the bed.

SLOW FADEOUT (Lights and sound)

109

SCENE 13

FADEUP

Janis' motel room showing her lying on the floor is dimly lit forming a backdrop to the final scene.

BACK PROJECTION:

<u>**Text**</u>**: 'October 1970'**
<u>**Image**</u>**: Any picture of Janis.**

Janis' mother Dorothy, dressed in black, is walking slowly across stage front under spots. A hotel receptionist appears and catches her up.

HOTEL CLERK

Er...excuse me, Mrs Joplin?

DOROTHY

Yes?

HOTEL CLERK

Er...sorry to bother you at this difficult time. Please...I'd like to offer my condolences. I...I was a fan...of your... It's...it's terrible...a great loss...for everyone.

DOROTHY

Yes. Thank you. I'm sure everyone must be devastated.

(She turns to go.)

HOTEL CLERK

Er...sorry... I've got this for you. It's addressed to...her...we...they weren't sure what to do with it.

(He holds out a letter. Dorothy just stares at it.)

I...I think it's from...well...obviously someone who knew her. It's a telegram. They said at the hotel...said they received it...yesterday. They didn't...well, obviously...somebody forgot about it, I suppose. They didn't get it to her...in time.

(The clerk stands there looking distraught. Dorothy takes the letter.)

DOROTHY

Thank you. I'll...thanks.

(The clerk exits hesitantly. Dorothy looks at the envelope in her hand, unsure what to do. After a while, she opens it. Video of Janis singing - 'Stay With Me' starts quietly on the back projection. The audience hears the contents of the letter as a voiceover in Jon's voice.)

'Hey Mama, its Jon. Missing you, babe. Meet you in Kathmandu? Love you, Mama. More than you know.'

SLOW FADE TO BLACK

OUTRO MUSIC: The video builds to full volume for the chorus and then slowly fades out.

CURTAIN